BIG TEST
JITTERS

Charlesbridge

Charlesbridge

BIG TEST JITTERS

JULIE DANNEBERG
ILLUSTRATED BY JUDY LOVE

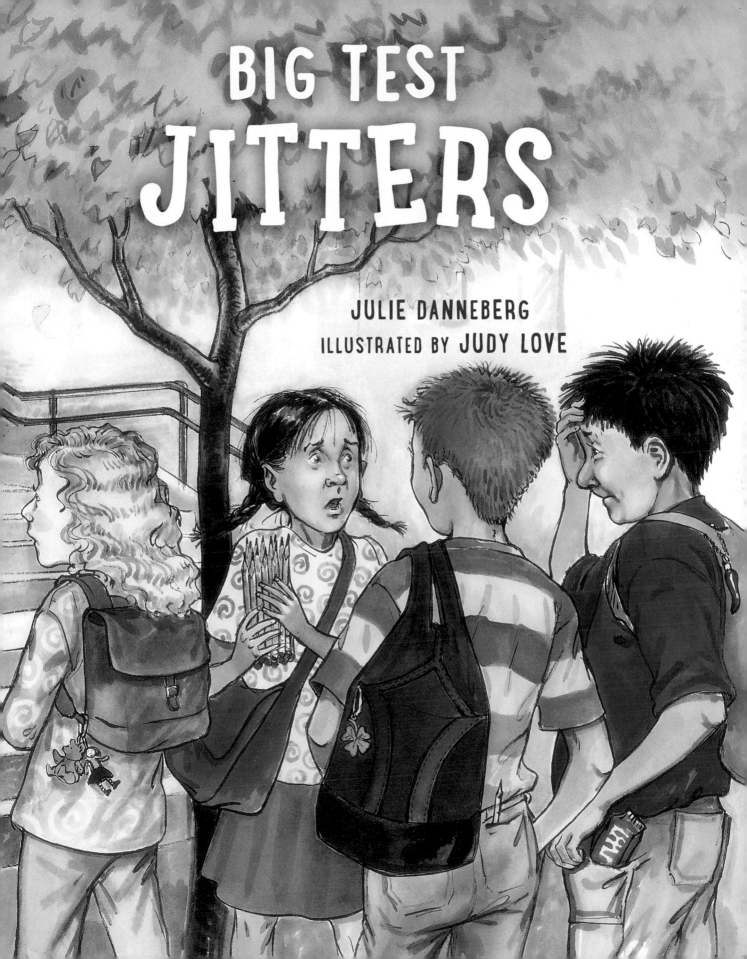

To my brothers: Dan, Ed, and Andy.
Thank you for your strength and presence
as we faced our own Big Test.
—J. D.

For Roger, who has been there for me
from the first scribbled sketches through
the final scans. With gratitude and love.
—J. L.

Text copyright © 2011 by Julie Danneberg
Illustrations copyright © 2011 by Judy Love
Originally published as *The Big Test*.
All rights reserved, including the right of reproduction in whole or in part in any form.
Charlesbridge and colophon are registered trademarks of Charlesbridge Publishing, Inc.

At the time of publication, all URLs printed in this book were accurate and active. Charlesbridge,
the author, and the illustrator are not responsible for the content or accessibility of any website.

Published by Charlesbridge, 9 Galen Street, Watertown, MA 02472
(617) 926-0329 • www.charlesbridge.com

Library of Congress Cataloging-in-Publication Data available upon request
ISBN 978-1-58089-073-1 (paperback)
ISBN 978-1-63289–674-2 (ebook)

Printed in China
(pb) 10 9 8 7 6 5 4 3 2

Illustrations done in ink and transparent dyes on Arches watercolor paper
Display type and text type set in LunchBox and Electra
Color separations by Chroma Graphics, Singapore
Printed by 1010 Printing International Limited in Huizhou, Guangdong, China
Cover design by Sara Gillingham; interior design by Diane M. Earley
Production supervision by Brian G. Walker

Mrs. Hartwell felt good.
Really good.
Really, really good.

All year long her students had worked hard,
learned lots, and had fun.

And now, as the school year neared its end, Mrs. Hartwell told her students that they were ready to take the Big Test.

"Yuck," said Eddie.

"Double yuck," said Alexandra.

"Double, triple, quadruple yuck,"
said Josh. "I hate tests."

Mrs. Hartwell laughed. "Don't worry, this test is
just a chance to show how much you've learned."

"Like addition," Emily shouted out.

$$
\begin{array}{r}
\overset{3}{5}7 \\
+\,42 \\
+\,16 \\
+\,28 \\
+\,39 \\
\hline
=182
\end{array}
$$

"And reading," said Maria.

"And science," Jack joined in.

Mrs. Hartwell nodded in agreement.

Leaning forward, she added, "We still have one thing left to learn, though."

The class was confused.

"But you just said we were ready," Daniel said.

"You are. Almost. But on a test you also have to
know
how to *show*
what you *know*,"
explained Mrs. Hartwell. "It's the last thing we
have to learn. It will be fun."

So during reading time that morning, Mrs. Hartwell sent the students straight to their seats. "Today we're going to practice our sitting-still-for-long-periods-of-time skill. I want you to read at your seat and work by yourself."

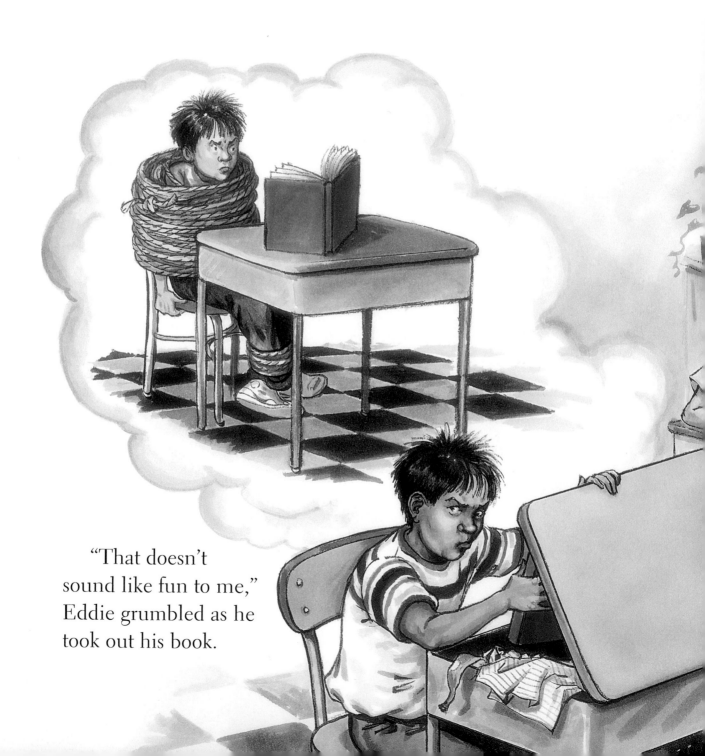

"That doesn't sound like fun to me," Eddie grumbled as he took out his book.

The class worked quietly. The reading part was easy. Sitting still without making a sound was hard. For Andy it was impossible.

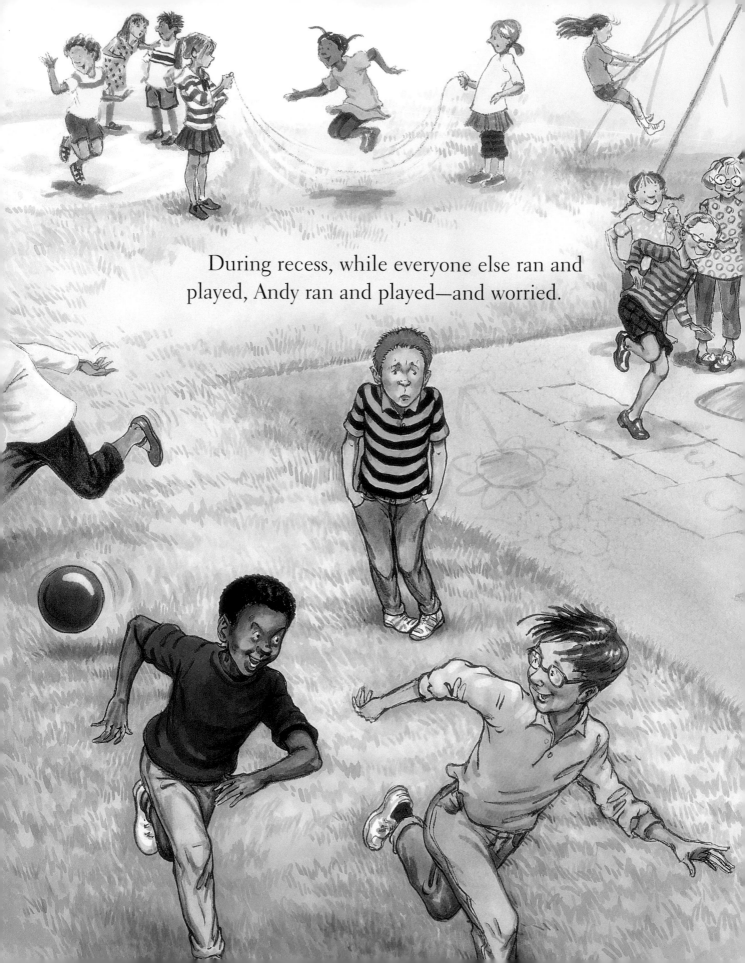

During recess, while everyone else ran and played, Andy ran and played—and worried.

After recess Andy's stomach hurt. He asked to
go to the nurse.

"Okay," said Mrs. Hartwell sadly, "but you'll be
missing this afternoon's let's-all-read-the-directions
lesson."

Andy didn't mind.

On Tuesday morning Mrs. Hartwell said,
"Friday is the day of the Big Test. Since we don't
want any bubble trouble when we take it, we're
going to practice our fill-in-the-bubble skills."

Everyone worked hard. Everyone did just
fine. Everyone, that is, except Emily and Maria.

By the time they were done working, Emily
had a headache, and Maria felt shivery all over.
They asked to go to the nurse.

"Okay," said Mrs. Hartwell, looking concerned,
"but you're going to miss our morning-of-the-test-
nutrition lesson."

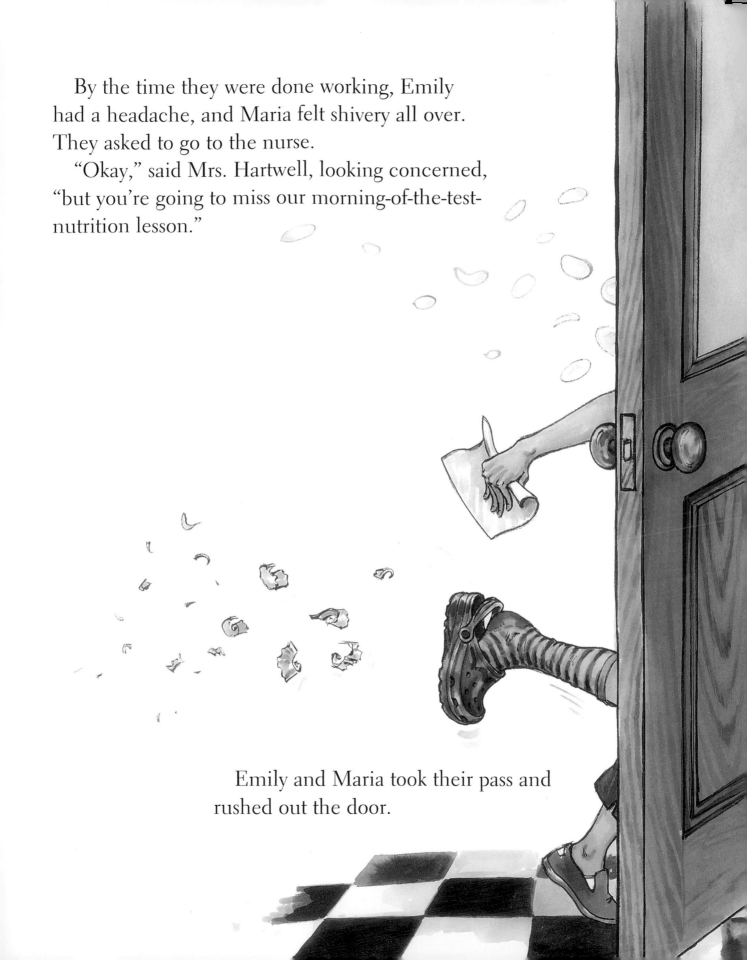

Emily and Maria took their pass and
rushed out the door.

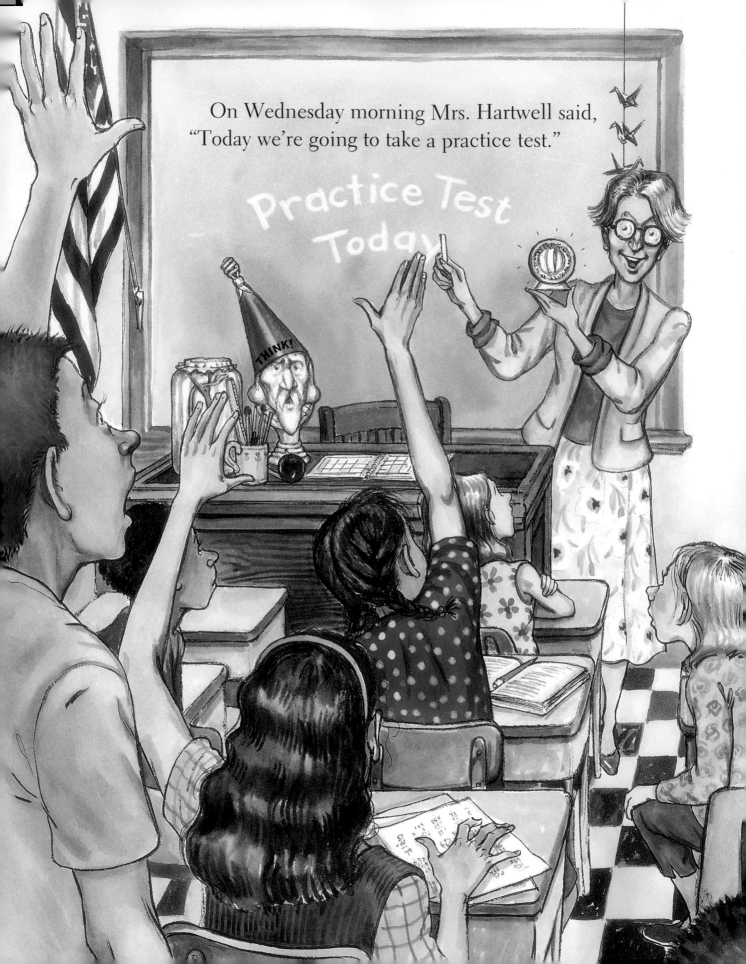

"Do we have to sit still for long periods of time?" asked Andy.

"Yes," said Mrs. Hartwell.

"Do we have to fill in bubbles?" asked Emily.

"And be sure to follow the directions?" asked Maria.

"Yes, you do." Mrs. Hartwell smiled encouragingly. "Remember, this test is a chance to show what you know . . . before the timer goes off."

Although most of the class did just fine, by the time the practice test was over, Daniel had gone to the nurse.

As Mrs. Hartwell watched him go, she felt bad. Really bad. Really, really bad.

On Wednesday afternoon, just before the bell, Mrs. Hartwell reminded everyone that tomorrow was the last day before the Big Test.

"We know, we know," Eddie said grumpily. "This Big Test is no fun. I can't wait for it to be over."

All the other students nodded in agreement.

As Mrs. Hartwell straightened up her desk, she said, "Tomorrow will be better, I promise."

When the students entered the classroom on Thursday, Mrs. Hartwell greeted them with a smile.

"You've all worked hard this year, learned lots, and had fun, right?" she asked.

"Yeah," said the class.

"And this week we practiced how to show what you know, right?"

"Right," said the class hesitantly.

"Now it's time for the most important lesson of all," said Mrs. Hartwell.

The class groaned as she told everyone to line up.

Mrs. Hartwell walked her students down the hall.
Everyone felt a little bit nervous.
Mrs. Hartwell walked her students right up
to the door of the library.
Everyone felt a *lot* nervous.

They gasped when she hung a sign on the library door.
"I feel sick," said Eddie.

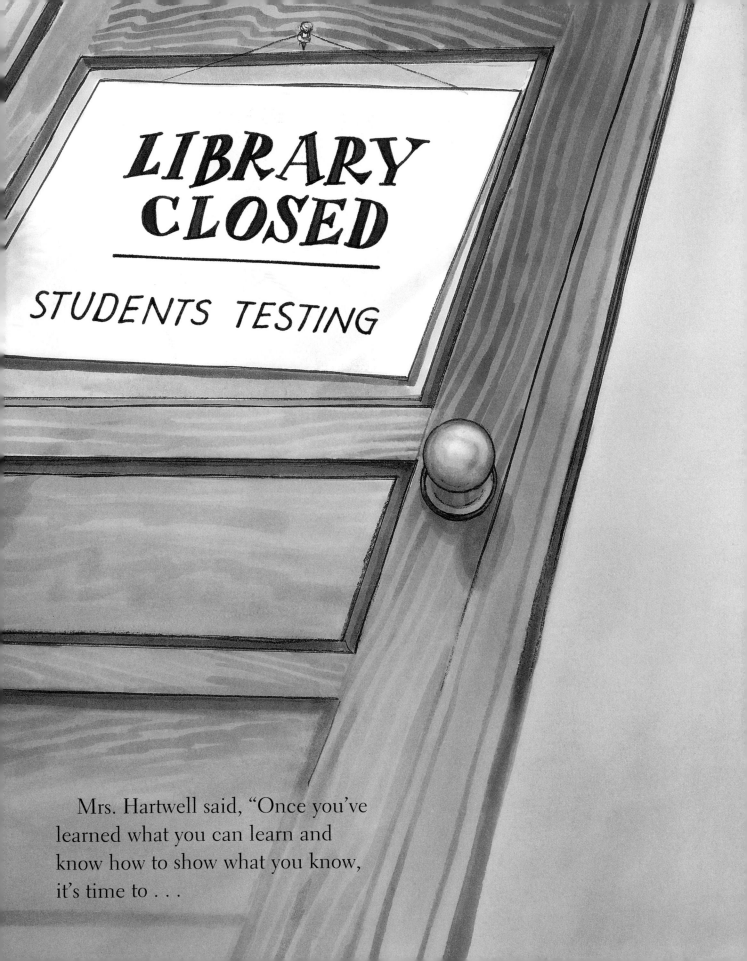

LIBRARY CLOSED

STUDENTS TESTING

Mrs. Hartwell said, "Once you've learned what you can learn and know how to show what you know, it's time to . . .

So the class did just that. And when the students finished the Big Test on Friday, they felt good.
Really good.
Really, really good.